SWAT
Secret World Adventure Team

Amazing
Africa

by
Lisa Thompson

illustrated by
Roger Harvey

PiCTURE WiNDOW BOOKS
Minneapolis, Minnesota

Editor: Jill Kalz
Page Production: Tracy Kaehler
Creative Director: Keith Griffin
Editorial Director: Carol Jones

First American edition published in 2006 by
Picture Window Books
5115 Excelsior Boulevard
Suite 232
Minneapolis, MN 55416
877-845-8392
www.picturewindowbooks.com

First published in Australia by
Blake Education Pty Ltd
CAN 074 266 023
Locked Bag 2022
Glebe NSW 2037
Ph: (02) 9518 4222; Fax: (02) 9518 4333
Email: mail@blake.com.au
www.askblake.com.au
© Blake Publishing Pty Ltd Australia 2005

Printed in the United States of America.

Library of Congress Cataloging-in-Publication Data
Thompson, Lisa, 1969-
Amazing Africa / by Lisa Thompson ; illustrated by
Roger Harvey.
p. cm. — (Read-it! chapter books. SWAT)
Summary: The Secret World Adventure Team recruits Sophie and
Matt as secret agents, then sends them to Kenya to help stop
some poachers who are killing elephants for their tusks.
ISBN 1-4048-1674-7 (hardcover)
[1. Poaching—Fiction. 2. Animal rescue—Fiction. 3. Elephants—
Fiction. 4. Adventure and adventurers—Fiction. 5. Kenya—
Fiction.] I. Harvey, Roger, 1962- ill. II. Title. III.
Series.
PZ7.T371634Ama 2005
[E]—dc22   2005027170

Table of Contents

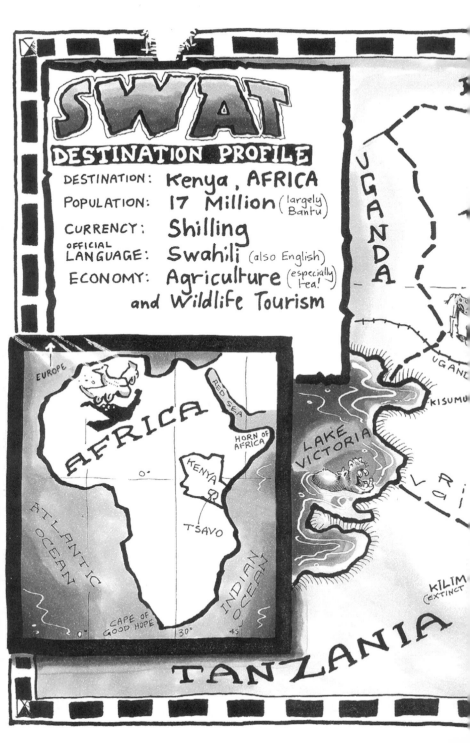

THIOPIA
KENYA
SOMALIA
N
W
S
S
MT KENYA
EQUATOR
0° LATITUDE
AIROBI
BASA RAILWAY
TSAVO NATIONAL PARK
TSAVO EAST
TSAVO WEST
tea
LAMU
INDIAN OCEAN
MOMBASA
RH

CHAPTER 1
The Mission

Matt and Sophie felt as if they had been walking forever.

"Matt, I think we'll throw our lines in here," said Sophie, throwing her huge backpack to the ground.

Matt dropped his backpack and ran to the water's edge. "This is a perfect spot," he said.

"Wonderful!" Sophie exclaimed. "I couldn't walk another step. This sun is boiling. I can't believe we lugged all of this stuff down here just to go fishing!" Sophie's face was bright red from the walk, and her shirt felt sticky.

"That water looks great," said Matt.

The water was crystal clear and made little waterfalls over the rocks.

"Let's go swimming first," said Sophie.

Matt didn't need too much convincing. He took off his shirt and jumped right in. "WWWWHHHHOOOOOEEEE!" he screamed. "It's really ...."

"COLD!" cried Sophie, who was already in the water.

They splashed around for a while, until
Matt hit his foot on something hard.
He saw something shiny on the bottom
of the river.

He bent down and picked it up. It was a silver container. On one side was the word "SWAT." The other side said:

TOP SECRET
ATTENTION MATT AND SOPHIE

Matt took the container to the riverbank, dried off, and got dressed. Sophie followed.

"It's weird that our names are on it,"
Matt said, as he tried to unscrew the
cap. "What do you think the word
'SWAT' stands for?"

Sophie shrugged. POP! The cap
opened. Out fell a small device flashing
the words "PLAY ME." Matt pressed
the **PLAY** button, and a voice started.

"Sophie and Matt, welcome to SWAT. SWAT is a top secret team whose name stands for Secret World Adventure Team. My name is Gosic. I am the voice of SWAT. We have a database of every child in the world. From this we choose our secret agents. Congratulations! We have chosen you for our next mission. We urgently need your help in Kenya, Africa.

"Your mission is to help Kenyan wildlife officer Sam Kimani Kariuki. Some of the elephants in his park are being hunted and killed by poachers.

"Inside this container are two transporter wristbands. You must wear these wristbands at all times. They allow you to travel in the blink of an eye, and they will keep us in contact. Tell no one you are SWAT agents. You must leave at once! Press **START MISSION** on the wristbands to begin your mission. Good luck, SWAT."

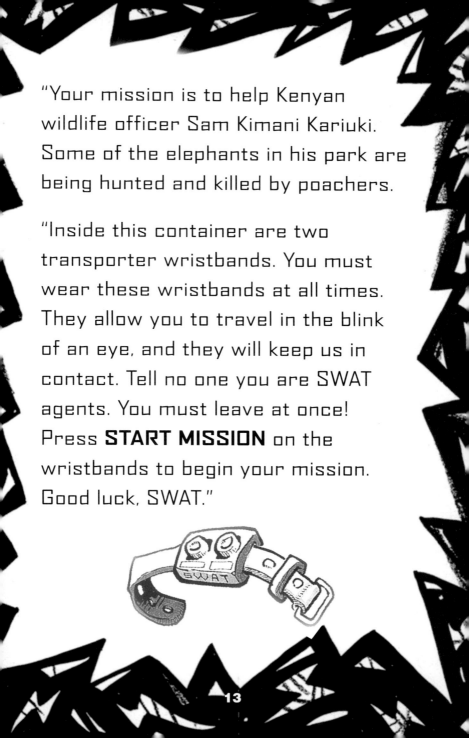

The voice stopped.

Matt passed a wristband to Sophie. "Here's one for you."

"Do you think it's a joke?" she asked.

"There is only one way to find out," Matt replied, as he put his on.

They didn't know much about Kenya, although Matt did know that its capital is Nairobi.

"Ready when you are," said Sophie.

They counted together.
"Three. Two. One."

Click.

START MISSION.

CHAPTER 2
Sam and Kibo

When they landed, people were running everywhere, yelling and screaming. Sophie and Matt heard a rumble getting closer and closer.

"Look out!" Matt cried, as a baby elephant charged past. It was being chased by villagers.

"It must be scared out of its mind," said Sophie.

The villagers were trying to force the elephant into a fenced-off pen. After much chasing, the elephant ran into the pen. Sophie and Matt went over to take a closer look.

17

"Where did you ...? How did you ...?"
a man said to them, looking confused.
"Never mind. You can tell me later.
Right now I need your help." He led
Sophie and Matt toward the captured
baby elephant.

The man wore a badge that said "Tsavo National Park Warden." His name was Sam Kimani Kariuki.

"Just call me Sam," he said with a smile. "I am the warden of Africa's biggest national park. This baby elephant is very distressed. Her mother was killed by poachers. Poachers kill elephants for their tusks and skin. The baby came into the village in search of food. She's not doing well. She's very weak and hungry."

Sam continued, "This is a Masai village. The Masai are famous warriors and herdsmen of Kenya. They don't like it when elephants scare away their livestock and damage their fences."

The village men were dressed in bright red cloth. The tall, beautiful women were covered in beaded jewelry. Necklaces curled around their necks and down their chests. Heavy earrings hung from their ears.

"What shall we call you, little
elephant?" asked Sam, scratching her
trunk. "Hmm, I know. We will call you
Kibo, after the peak of Africa's highest
mountain, Mount Kilimanjaro. With a
name like that, you will grow up big
and strong."

A park worker handed Sam a huge
baby bottle. "We do not have a lot of
formula," she said. "We will have to
move her soon."

"Move her where?" asked Matt and Sophie together.

"Kibo needs to be looked after," the park worker said. "She is too young to take care of herself. She will not survive in the wild. Elephants live in herds, and now that little Kibo's herd is gone, she will not be safe alone. I have a friend who looks after orphaned animals. We will take Kibo there tomorrow morning."

Sam passed the bottle to Sophie and said, "We need you two to feed her and keep her company. Give her lots of attention, and don't leave her alone. I will go and tell the villagers what we are planning to do."

Kibo was much happier now that she had been fed. She flicked her ears back and forth and wrapped her trunk tightly around Matt's wrist.

"Thanks, Kibo. I like you, too." Matt rubbed the top of her head.

Kibo squeezed him tighter.

"OK, OK, that's tight enough. Let go, Kibo." As hard as he tried, Matt couldn't uncurl himself from Kibo's trunk.

"Way to go, Kibo. Let him know who's boss," giggled Sophie.

Sam returned with some blankets.
"These are for you, so you can sleep
with Kibo. Put one around her, too. I
will come and get you in the morning."

As the sun faded, Sophie, Matt, and Kibo curled up under their blankets. Kibo loved it. She was used to sleeping with a herd. Every so often she would twitch and lift her trunk as though she was having a bad dream. Sophie or Matt would get up, pat her on the head, and say, "It's OK, Kibo. You're safe now." And Kibo would fall asleep again.

CHAPTER 3
The Dawn of a Big Day

When they woke, the sun was just peeking over the horizon. Sophie looked around. The ground was dry and red. The flat grassland seemed to go on for miles. Dotted here and there were trees and animals.

All of the village huts were made of mud and had grass roofs to keep them cool. The village was quiet. The villagers were out tending to their herds of cattle. Life seemed to move slowly in Kenya.

Kibo, Sophie, and Matt got to their feet and stretched. Kibo shook her head and flapped her ears.

"Hello," said a voice on the other side of the fence. "Did you sleep well with the baby elephant?" The voice belonged to a Masai boy, about the same age as Matt.

Matt was brushing the dust off himself. "Yes, thanks. Does everyone always get up so early here?"

"It is good to do work before it gets too hot," replied the Masai boy. "And there is much work to do. The baby elephant did a lot of damage when she ran through the village yesterday. We have had many wild animals scaring our herds lately. They run through the village trying to get away from the poachers and their guns.

"Baby elephants are funny aren't they?" the boy continued, holding out his hand.

"Sam named her Kibo," said Sophie.

Kibo wasn't so sure about the boy. Maybe she remembered him from yesterday. Elephants have very good memories. She lifted her trunk to smell. The boy said something to Kibo.

"What did you just say?" asked Matt.

safari

"I was talking to Kibo in Swahili. Swahili is the official language of Kenya. I know a Swahili word that you will know— 'safari.' It's Swahili for 'expedition.'"

When Sam showed up, Kibo raised her trunk and let out a rumble.

"Today, you are going on an adventure," Sam said softly to Kibo.

Sam had brought a truck with him to transport Kibo. Kibo sniffed the truck and felt it with her trunk. Sam smiled and pointed to Sophie and Matt.

"You two will have to ride in the back of the truck," Sam said, "so Kibo won't get too scared."

Sophie and Matt made getting on the truck a game for Kibo. She ran up the ramp, chasing Matt as he held her breakfast bottle. Once the elephant was in the truck, Sam passed Matt a big bottle of sunscreen.

"Put this on Kibo so she doesn't get sunburned. A baby elephant's skin is very sensitive. She'd usually roll around in the mud and the dirt to cover her skin. Today we'll have to use sunscreen," Sam explained.

Kibo thought it was great being rubbed
all over. She kept trying to rub them
back, pushing her rump onto their
clothes. It was a very messy job. By the
time they were finished, all three of
them were covered with sunscreen.

CHAPTER 4
The Wildlife Orphanage

They drove for half the day. At last they came to the Wildlife Orphanage. It was like an open park that went on forever. Elephants of all sizes were roaming around. In the middle was a small house. Kibo poked her head over the side of the truck.

"This looks like a pretty good place, Kibo," said Sophie.

One of the younger elephants made a loud rumble like she was saying hello. Kibo rumbled back. Once Kibo was free, the two young elephants ran to greet each other.

"I wonder if they know each other," said Sophie.

"Could be," said Sam. "I picked the other elephant up not far from where we found Kibo. It looks like they're from the same herd."

"Hello, Sam," said a woman standing on the porch. "Another orphaned elephant? When is it going to stop?" she asked, shaking her head. "I see you have some new helpers."

Matt stepped forward. "My name is Matt, and this is Sophie."

"My name is Cynthia," the woman said.

"Cynthia is an elephant expert," said Sam. "She helps baby elephants get fit and strong. Then she helps them return to life in the wild."

"Come inside," said Cynthia. "I want you to meet someone."

The house was filled with carvings and furniture with big cushions.

"That looks comfortable!" said Matt, pointing to the couch. "Not like last night with Kibo."

"Ahhh! You slept with her last night," said Cynthia. "That is good. Kibo will need 24-hour attention for some time so she doesn't get lonely. Elephants can die of loneliness, you know."

Cynthia saw the look on Sophie's face when she said that. "Don't worry, Sophie. Kibo will be fine here."

Cynthia looked around. "Now, I wonder where our friend has run off to? Wait here. Make yourselves at home. We'll be back in a moment." She took Sam with her.

Matt dove for the couch.

"Matt!" cried Sophie.

"Well, she did say make yourself at home!" Matt said.

Sophie looked at the bookcase. It was filled with books about elephants. Some of them looked really old. Cynthia must really know her stuff, Sophie thought. That made Sophie feel much better. Suddenly, Sophie felt someone staring at her. She slowly turned around.

A man was standing at the door. He stood very straight and had a strong stare like that of a lion. Matt and Sophie could tell he was someone important. He didn't look happy.

"There you are," said Cynthia. "Sam and I have been looking for you."

"G.K., my good friend," said Sam, giving the man a warm handshake.

"Sophie and Matt, this is Galogola Kafonde. We call him G.K. He is from the Waliangulu tribe. For hundreds of years, the Waliangulu tribe were the best elephant hunters in Africa. G.K.'s grandfather was a very famous hunter.

"The tribe cannot live that life anymore, but they are still supreme bushman. G.K. is the best elephant tracker there is. He lives in a small village in Tsavo and guards the elephants. By the look on your face, G.K., you bring us bad news."

G.K. looked sad as he told his news.

"This morning we found two more dead elephants as well as a dead rhino. I have just found fresh poacher tracks not far from here. They seem to be following the herd that your new baby elephant belongs to."

"We must leave at once," said Sam.

"You can take the plane," said Cynthia.

"We're coming with you," said Matt and Sophie. "We want to help."

Sam looked surprised, but there was no time to argue.

CHAPTER 5
Hunting the Poachers

Sam, Sophie, Matt, and G.K. boarded the tiny plane. Sam called the other park rangers. They were to meet at the riverbank where the elephants had last been seen. Sam would keep in radio contact and tell them exactly where the elephants were.

"Belt up," said Sam, as he started the plane's engine. They bumped along the dusty runway.

They left the ground, and the land beneath them fell away. Tall baobab trees now looked tiny. Everyone in the plane scanned the ground for elephants and poachers.

Sam gave Matt and Sophie some binoculars. "These will make spotting them easier," he said.

They flew over herds of zebras, giraffes, and wildebeest. They saw hippos lying in the mud and vultures waiting on branches for their next meal. They even spotted a group of lions.

The sun was sizzling now, and there wasn't a cloud in the sky. The only shadow on the ground came from the little plane.

Matt spotted the herd
of elephants first.

"I can't see any
poachers yet,"
yelled Matt. "Wait! I
think I do see something."

"It's their camp," said G.K. "It looks
like they must be out hunting. They'll
be back, though."

"I'll land the plane not far from here,
and we'll walk in," said Sam.

They landed and started walking. They could see signs of where the elephants had been. Branches were half-stripped of their leaves, and large elephant tracks covered the ground. Elephant droppings appeared here and there.

"Make sure you don't step in that, Matt," said Sophie. "Or we'll have to send out a search party!"

"Sam," Matt asked, "why do poachers kill elephants? Aren't they afraid of getting caught by the police?"

"Some people in Kenya are very poor," said Sam. "It is illegal to kill elephants. You can go to jail. People still do it because you can make a lot of money selling elephant tusks. People want the ivory. A poacher can make more money from one elephant than he can working a year in Kenya."

CHAPTER 6
The Ambush

They could see the herd of elephants in the distance. The elephants were red from the dust. Some of them were rolling in the dirt. Others were playing in the water.

"Elephants don't have sweat glands, so they cool off in the water," Sam said. He pointed to the biggest elephant. "That's Zena. She's the leader. Every elephant herd has a leader."

Zena lifted her trunk in the air.

"Get down," said G.K. "We don't want her noticing us."

The elephants were having a great time rumbling, trumpeting, and roaring. They looked huge. Their trunks were curling, swaying, and lifting water to spray on their backs.

"They look so beautiful," said Sophie. "I can't believe anyone would want to kill them for their tusks."

One of the rangers from the truck appeared with news from the poachers' camp. The poachers had returned. They had been hunting lions and now looked like they were getting ready to hunt Zena and her herd.

"We must hurry," said Sam. "We must make it in time."

Matt and Sophie looked at their transporter wristbands.

"Sophie, you grab Sam's hand, and I'll grab G.K.'s," said Matt. "Ready? Three. Two. One."

Click.

They landed just outside the poachers' camp. G.K. shook his head and gave Matt a bewildered stare.

Sam said, "I have no idea how you did that!" He looked through the binoculars. "The poachers are getting ready for the elephant hunt."

Sam saw that the other rangers were in position. He gave the signal. They all ran into the camp together.

The poachers were caught off guard. They had nowhere to run. Sam and his team arrested seven men. It was a perfect result. Or so they thought.

CHAPTER 7
Saving Zena

G.K. knelt on the ground. He saw fresh tracks.

"One of the poachers has already left."

Matt grabbed G.K. and hit his transporter button. "We'll beat him!" he said. "Three. Two. One."

Click.

They reached the poacher just as he was kneeling down. The poacher lifted his gun and prepared to shoot. It was a terrifying sight.

Zena and her elephants sensed trouble. Her trunk flared up, and she let out an almighty roar. She charged straight at the poacher and his gun. The rest of the adult elephants were charging right behind her.

Matt and G.K. leapt for the poacher. G.K. grabbed his rifle and wrestled him to the ground.

"AHHHHHHHHHHHHH! Get your hands off me!" yelled the poacher.

G.K. held the poacher as tightly as he could. "You're not going anywhere. You're under arrest."

Zena and her herd were approaching fast. She was angry.

"Let's gooooo!" yelled Matt.

He hit the transporter button as quickly as he could. They got out of Zena's way just in time, landing a safe distance away. The three of them watched the herd come to a stop. Zena sniffed the area where the poacher had been lying. She lifted her leg and stomped the ground in anger.

"I wouldn't go back there if I were you," said Matt to the poacher. "An elephant never forgets your smell."

When they got back to Sam and Sophie, Sam was beaming. "I don't know how you did that, Matt, but thanks. You and G.K. saved Zena and her entire herd."

"Will it be safe for Kibo to join them again, now?" asked Sophie excitedly.

"When she is stronger," said Sam. "Now let's get this guy on the truck with the others."

G.K. turned to Matt and Sophie. "You two make great warriors," he said. "There used to be a big celebration in my tribe when you killed your first elephant. Now it is a great day when you save one. Today you both became warriors. You showed real courage."

Matt and Sophie turned to watch Zena and her herd playing in the water hole.

"They look so happy, don't they?" said Sophie.

Zena let out a mighty roar and flicked her trunk, spraying water everywhere.

Matt and Sophie felt their wristbands vibrate. Sophie looked down and read the message from Gosic:

Well done, SWAT! Mission successful. Congratulations.

A red button appeared on their wristbands marked **MISSION RETURN**.

CHAPTER 8
Leaving Africa

Sam called them over. "Time to get on the plane, you two."

He radioed ahead to tell Cynthia the good news. When they landed, she ran to the plane with congratulations.

"Fantastic job!" she cried. "I've put together a little party to celebrate."

There were tables in front of the house piled with food. The elephant keepers were dancing and singing traditional tribal songs. Everyone was having a wonderful time.

Sam thanked everyone for their help and then made an announcement: "Matt and Sophie, I officially declare you both honorary park wardens of Tsavo National Park, Kenya."

Everyone cheered. Sophie and Matt were delighted. Cynthia ran inside.

"You never did tell me how you move around so quickly!" said Sam.

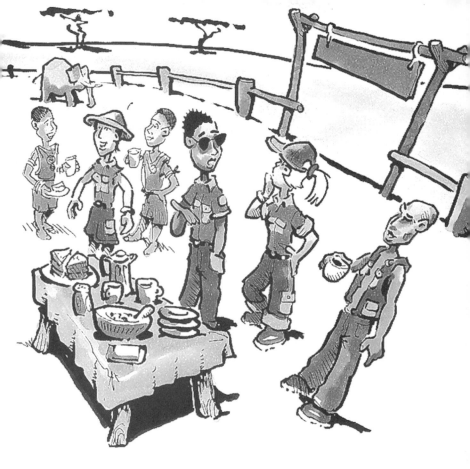

Just then, Cynthia returned with a cake and presents. Matt and Sophie didn't have to answer Sam's question.

"Open them later," Cynthia whispered.

Everyone started singing, dancing, and eating again.

Matt and Sophie felt their wristbands vibrate for a second time. This time the **MISSION RETURN** button was flashing.

"It's really time for us to leave," said Matt quietly to Sophie.

"OK, just one minute," she said, running over to Kibo.

Sophie scratched Kibo's trunk and rubbed the animal's head.

"Good-bye, little Kibo. You'll be safe now. Stay out of trouble," Sophie said.

Kibo let out a little screech, and the other elephants answered.

"Let's open these presents," said Matt, ripping his open as he spoke.

Sophie wasn't far behind. Inside each package was a T-shirt that read:

ONLY ELEPHANTS SHOULD
WEAR IVORY

"What do you think, Kibo?" Matt asked.

Kibo and the other elephants let out a rumble as though they knew what it said.

"Let's go, Matt," Sophie said. "We've got some fish to catch. You might be an expert at catching elephant poachers, but let's see how good you are at catching fish!"

Matt pounded his chest and said, "I'm a mighty warrior. I can catch anything!"

"Not with your foot in that big pile of elephant poop!" laughed Sophie. "Three. Two. One."

Click.

MISSION RETURN.

GLOSSARY

almighty—huge, enormous

baobab trees—wide-trunked trees native to Africa

device—a gadget

expedition—an adventure

formula—a milk drink given to babies

horizon—where the earth meets the sky

ivory—elephants' tusks are made of this hard, white material

Kenya—a country in Africa

livestock—animals bred and sold to make money

Masai—a tribe in Africa

off guard—surprised

orphaned—to not have a mother or a father

poachers—people who hunt animals illegally

Swahili—the official language of Kenya

tribal—to do with a tribe

warden—a caretaker

warrior—a brave fighter

wildebeest—antelope-like animals native to Africa